MY HAUNTED HOUSE

ALSO BY
ANGIE SAGE

ARAMINTA SPOOK 2:
The Sword in the Grotto

SEPTIMUS HEAP, BOOK ONE:
Magyk

SEPTIMUS HEAP, BOOK TWO:
Flyte

-1-
ARAMINTA SPOOK

MY HAUNTED HOUSE

as told to
ANGIE SAGE

illustrated by
JIMMY PICKERING

BLOOMSBURY

First published in Great Britain in 2006 by Bloomsbury Publishing Plc,
36 Soho Square, London W1D 3QY

Published in America by HarperCollins Children's Books,
a division of HarperCollins Publishers, 1350 Avenue of the Americas,
New York NY 10019

Text copyright © Angie Sage 2006
Illustrations copyright © Jimmy Pickering 2006
The moral rights of the author and illustrator have been asserted

A CIP catalogue record of this book is available from the British Library

ISBN 0 7475 8346 3
ISBN-13 9780747583462

All papers used by Bloomsbury Publishing are natural, recyclable products
made from wood grown in well-managed forests. The manufacturing processes
conform to the environmental regulations of the country of origin.

Printed in Italy by L.E.G.O.S.p.A

1 3 5 7 9 10 8 6 4 2

www.aramintaspook.co.uk

For
Araminta Clibborn,
with love

CONTENTS

MY HAUNTED HOUSE

~1~
SIR HORACE'S HELMET

It all began when I was in my Thursday bedroom doing my ghost practice. I have always done regular ghost practice, as I was sure it would be much easier to find a ghost if the ghost thought that I was one too. I have always wanted to find a ghost, but you know, even though our house is called Spook House, I have never, ever seen a single ghost, not even a very small one. I thought that Aunt

Tabby had scared them off—she would scare me off if I were a ghost.

Anyway, I was busy doing my practice and I had my ghost sheet over my head, which is why I tripped over Sir Horace's left foot. Stupid thing. And then his left foot fell off, and Sir Horace collapsed into hundreds of

pieces. Stupid Sir Horace. And then all the bits of stupid Sir Horace rolled all over the floor, and I stepped on his head and got my foot stuck inside it. Don't worry, it wasn't a *real* head. Sir Horace is just a boring old suit of armour that's always hanging around here, lurking in various dark corners.

I was yelling at it to get *off* and hopping around shaking my foot like mad, but Sir Horace's stupid head was totally stuck. Then, with really great timing, Aunt Tabby shouted, "Breakfast!" in that if-you-don't-come-down-right-now-and-get-it-I-shall-give-it-to-the-cat voice—not that we have a cat, but she would if we did have one, I know she would.

So I gave my foot the biggest shake ever—in fact, I am surprised my whole leg didn't come off—and Sir Horace's helmet flew off, shot out of the bedroom door, and hurtled down the attic stairs. It made a fantastic noise. I could hear it all the way down to the basement. Sound travels really well in this house, so I could easily hear Aunt Tabby's scream, too.

I thought I'd better get going, so I slid down the banister and hopped off at the landing. I wanted to see if Uncle Drac had gone to sleep yet—he works nights— because if he had, I was going to wake him up and make him come downstairs with me just in case Aunt Tabby was going to throw a wobbly. His bedroom door is the little red one at the end of the top corridor, the one that goes to the turret.

I was very careful pushing the door open, as it's a sheer drop down for miles. Uncle Drac took all the floors out of the turret so that his bats could fly wherever they wanted. Uncle Drac loves his bats; he'd do anything for them. I love bats too. They are *so* sweet.

I pushed Big Bat out of the way, and he fell all the way down to the bottom of the turret. It didn't matter, though, as the floor of the turret is about ten feet deep in bat poo, so it's very soft.

Without Big Bat clogging up the door, I could easily see Uncle Drac's sleeping bag. It was hanging from one of the joists like a great big flowery bat—and it was empty. Great, I thought, he's still downstairs with Aunt Tabby. So, to save time, I slid down the big stairs' banister and the basement stairs' banister too—which I'm not meant to do as it keeps falling over—and I was outside the second-kitchen-on-the-left-just-past-the-larder in no

time. It was suspiciously quiet in there. Oops, I thought, trouble.

I pushed open the door really considerately, and I was glad I did as Aunt Tabby was sitting at the end of the long table, buttering some toast in a way that made you think the toast had said something really personal and rude. It didn't look like a fun breakfast time, I thought. The signs were not good.

First not-good sign: sitting in the middle of the table was Sir Horace's helmet. It had a lot more dents in it than when I last saw it, but that was obviously not *my* fault as it was OK when it left my foot.

Second, third, fourth and fifth not-good signs: Aunt Tabby was covered in soot—apart from two little windows in her glasses which she had wiped clear so that she could attack the toast. Aunt Tabby being covered in soot is one of the worst signs. It means she has had a fight with the boiler and the boiler has won.

I sat down in my seat in a thoughtful and caring way. Uncle Drac looked really relieved to see me. You see, I live with my aunt and uncle because my parents went vampire hunting in Transylvania when I was little and they never came back.

Uncle Drac was busy scraping out the last bit of his boiled egg. He had soot all around his mouth from the sooty toast that Aunt Tabby had buttered for him.

"Hello, Minty," he said.

"Hello, Uncle Drac," I said. I tried to think of something nice to say to Aunt Tabby, but it was difficult to think of anything at all with Sir Horace's helmet staring at me with its little beady eyes. It doesn't really have eyes, of course, but I often used to think it was looking at me, even though I was sure it was nothing more than an empty tin can.

Aunt Tabby plonked my bowl of porridge down in front of me, so I said, "Thank you, Aunt Tabby." And then, because Aunt Tabby likes polite conversation at breakfast, I said, "Have you been having trouble with the boiler again, Aunt Tabby?"

"Yes, dear—but *not* for very much longer," Aunt Tabby said, hardly moving her lips. I

used to think that when Aunt Tabby spoke like that she was practising to be a ventriloquist, but now I know it means she has made her mind up about something and she doesn't care whether you agree with her or not.

"Oh, why is that, Aunt Tabby?" I asked especially nicely, while I covered my porridge with brown sugar and stirred it all in really fast so that the porridge went a nice muddy colour.

Aunt Tabby sort of gritted her teeth and said, *"Don't* do that with the sugar dear. Because we're *moving,* that's why."

Not much stops me digging mud ditches in my porridge—you know, the ones where you scrape a channel through it and it fills up with runny brown sugar, which I think looks just like mud—but that did.

Moving? What was she talking about? We couldn't possibly move, not before I'd found at least one ghost. And I wanted to find a vampire and a werewolf, too. I was sure there must be some in the cellar.

"Don't leave your mouth open when it is full, dear," said Aunt Tabby, which I didn't think was fair as Uncle Drac had *his* mouth open too, and it was full of sooty toast, which looked disgusting.

Then Aunt Tabby fixed Uncle Drac with her Fiendish Stare (which is nearly as good as mine) and said, "Drac, this house is far too big for us. It is *dusty* and it is *dirty*, it is *freezing*

cold and *full* of *spiders*. The boiler is a *menace*. We are moving to a nice, small, clean, modern flat *without a boiler*."

"*But*—" I tried to interrupt, but it was no use. Aunt Tabby just kept on going.

"And when we have moved to a flat, helmets from rusty old suits of armour won't keep landing on my toes, because we won't *have* any rusty old suits of armour. Sir Horace can go to the recycling bin. You can take him, Drac."

"What?" said Uncle Drac, looking a bit like one of my old goldfish used to look when the water in the fish bowl got very low.

At last I got a word in, even though I still had a mouthful of porridge, which I had been too shocked to swallow. "But we *can't* leave this house," I told Aunt Tabby. "*Nowhere* would ever be the same as this!"

"Exactly," said Aunt Tabby, like I'd agreed with her or something. "Nowhere could possibly be like this."

I looked at Uncle Drac—I needed some help here. Uncle Drac took the hint.

"Now, now, Tabby dear," he murmured in his calm-down-Aunt-Tabby voice, "you know you don't mean it."

"I *do* mean it, Drac," Aunt Tabby told him. Then she tried to get me on her side. "And, Araminta dear, you often say you're lonely here. Just think, you would have lots of friends in a nice block of flats."

She didn't succeed. "I don't care," I told her. "I'd rather stay here than have a lot of stupid friends anyway."

"Well, we will see about that," said Aunt Tabby, with her mad ventriloquist look.

~2~

THIS HOUSE IS FOR SALE

L ater that morning I was looking out of my Thursday bedroom window and thinking about what Aunt Tabby had said. I always find it easier to think when I am doing something, so I was busy picking off lumps of peeling black paint from around the windows and throwing them at the monster statues out on the parapet.

It was lucky that I looked down and

noticed the man standing on the front doorstep. He was wearing a shiny blue suit and was staring up at the house while he wrote down notes on his clipboard. I knew what he was straight away—an estate agent. I could see Aunt Tabby meant business.

Well, so did I.

So I got down from the window and hummed a happy tune to myself: "La-di-da, la-di-da, time to clean out the fish bowl." I found the old bowl in a dark corner, where I had put it after Brian, my last goldfish, escaped. I don't know where Brian went, but he never came back. For sentimental reasons I had kept the bowl just as Brian had left it, so it was full of slime, old weeds and some very smelly green water.

The estate agent was standing right

underneath my window. I balanced the fish bowl on the windowsill and tipped it. The sludge landed *splat* right on him. Bull's-eye!

The estate agent had green goo all over his head and his shiny blue suit. He just stood there for a moment—like he was really surprised—and spat out some bits of slippery weed. Then he looked up, and I aimed my Fiendish Stare at him.

He made a weird, spluttery, yelping noise and ran off down the path.

Good riddance.

At lunchtime in the third-kitchen-on-the-right-just-round-the-corner-past-the-boiler-room, I was not surprised to see that Aunt Tabby looked just as grumpy as she had at breakfast.

"These estate agents are really *most* unreliable," she said as she stabbed a defenceless potato and thumped it down on my plate. "I have been waiting all morning for one, but he hasn't even bothered to turn up."

I didn't say anything. Aunt Tabby looked at me for a moment and then she said, "I shall put my own sign up this afternoon. You'll enjoy helping me paint it, Araminta."

"Won't," I told her.

I tried to avoid Aunt Tabby in the afternoon, but she found me down in the cellar looking for vampires and dragged me out to the garden.

"It's a lovely day, Araminta," she burbled. "Some sunshine would do you good. You are looking quite pale."

Well, of course I was looking pale. It was because of the chalk dust all over my face. Vampire hunting is the same as ghost hunting—you have to look like one of them to have any chance of finding one. I think I look pretty good as a vampire, although I would like to grow my teeth, too (but when I asked the dentist how I could do that, she was not exactly helpful).

Aunt Tabby had cleared a patch of stinging

nettles—stinging nettles are what grow best in our garden—and she had dumped down a piece of board and some old paints. Aunt Tabby thinks she's an artist, but I have my doubts.

"Come on, dear," she said, patting the ground beside her like we were going to have a picnic or something, "you know you love painting."

"Don't," I told her.

So I sat on the steps and kicked them, which is quite fun as they are very crumbly and you can often get big lumps of stone to drop off. I watched Aunt Tabby really go for the paint in a big way until she had covered herself in as much paint as she had put on the board. When she had run out of paint, Aunt Tabby fixed the board to a post and stuck it in the hedge.

The sign said:

This
House
Is
for Sale

Aunt Tabby looked pleased. She rubbed her painty hands all down the front of her dress and said, "Not too bad. I haven't lost my touch. What do you think, Araminta?"

I didn't say what I thought, as it would not have been polite. Also I was thinking hard. I badly needed a Plan—Aunt Tabby was not going to get away with this. So while Aunt Tabby went indoors to shout at the boiler, I thought about my Plan. It didn't take long before I had one. Soon the sign said:

Simple.

~3~
HUGE HOTELS

The next morning I was up early. I knew Aunt Tabby was not going to give up easily and I wanted to keep an eye on her, so after breakfast I hung around the hall, pretending to count the spiders. Everything (even Aunt Tabby) was suspiciously quiet—until there was a knock on the door.

I rushed to open it, but Aunt Tabby, who had been lurking behind the clock, got there first. She elbowed me out of the way (Aunt Tabby has really sharp elbows) and opened the door.

Standing on the doorstep was a very stylish woman carrying a briefcase. I did not like the look of her one bit, so I did my best Fiendish Stare. I could tell it worked—she suddenly went very pale and gulped a bit like Brian used to. She opened and closed her mouth as though she had forgotten how to talk, and then she said in a squeaky voice, "I—I've come to see the house. On behalf of Huge Hotels Incorporated."

Aunt Tabby looked thrilled.

Drat, I thought. It was just my luck that this Huge Hotels person couldn't read. I stomped outside to check the sign, but it now said:

This
House
Is ~~NOT~~
For Sale

Hmm . . . Aunt Tabby was proving more tricky than I had expected.

She was busy showing Huge Hotels around the hall when I clomped back inside.

"It's very odd, dear," Aunt Tabby said with a funny kind of smile. "Someone changed the sign last night. I noticed it when Uncle Drac went to work. I wouldn't be surprised if it was one of those estate agents. Anyway, I've fixed it now, don't you think?"

I didn't reply—there was no time to lose. I tore upstairs to my Friday bedroom and grabbed my Ghost Kit. I threw open the box and pulled out my white ghost sheet and emptied a bag of flour over it. Then I blew up a big balloon and put in one of my surprise-your-friends-with-a-strangled-ghost squealers. I held on to the neck of the balloon really tightly to stop the air escaping, then I put the floury sheet over my head so that it covered me and the balloon.

I was ready.

Soon I could hear Aunt Tabby clumping up the stairs in her big boots, followed by Huge Hotels's scared little clip-clop sounds.

It was time to go.

I opened my bedroom door, and in the old mirror on the landing I could see a small, fat, dusty ghost shuffling out. I didn't look as scary as I had hoped, but it was pretty good. It was very difficult going down the attic stairs, but I managed to reach the bottom. Then I climbed on to the old chest by the landing window and hid behind the curtains.

Yes! The ambush was set.

I could hear Aunt Tabby and Huge Hotels Incorporated just along the corridor. Aunt Tabby was rattling on about how she personally *liked* the dripping taps in the bathroom, and Huge Hotels was muttering stuff to herself: "Great potential . . . Old world charm . . . Theme hotel . . ."

We'll see about *that*, I thought. I jumped off the chest and let go of the squealer.

Aiiieeeeeeeeeeeeeeeeeeee!

It was great. Huge Hotels went totally

pale. I could tell that she knew she had made a Big Mistake. She spun round and screamed. *Really* screamed. While she was screaming, I hung on to the curtains and waved my arms a

lot so that the flour flew all over the place like a thick white mist. The strangled-ghost squealer was great—it kept on squealing and squealing—but just to make sure of things, I made some really horrible groans, too.

Huge Hotels was not giving up easily. Her screams were amazing—really piercing—and she didn't stop, not even to breathe. Aunt Tabby grabbed hold of Huge Hotels to try and calm her down, but Huge Hotels didn't want to calm down. No way.

Just then some flour got stuck in my throat and made me choke a bit—well, quite a lot, actually—and that was when Huge Hotels stopped screaming and just stared at me, although she still had her mouth open like she wanted to scream.

She started inching slowly backwards

along the corridor and went straight through one of the oldest cobwebs, where the biggest, hairiest spiders live—and I saw the biggest, hairiest spider of them all fall down her front. Huge Hotels let out a piercing shriek that made my ears ring. She tore down the stairs and was out of the front door in two seconds flat.

I was impressed. "That was fast," I said, throwing off my sheet and taking a breath of flour-free air.

Aunt Tabby looked cross. "Really, Araminta, what *are* you doing?" she said. "I don't know what's got into you. Is that my best self-raising flour you've been using?"

"Yes," I told her. "But it didn't work. My feet didn't leave the ground once."

Aunt Tabby tut-tutted and scooped up the

spiders that had fallen off their cobwebs and got covered with flour. Then she carried them down to the kitchens to dust them off.

I sat by the mouldy curtains in the middle of a pile of flour and unwrapped my ghost sheet. Things were going well, I thought, but I knew Aunt Tabby was not going to give up that easily.

That evening, after Aunt Tabby had read me a story from *The Bedtime Ghouls and Ghosties Pink Storybook* and gone downstairs to feed the boiler, I got up. I crept down the attic stairs and waited in the shadows outside Uncle Drac's turret.

When the moon rose, the red door creaked open and Uncle Drac shuffled out. I watched him walk slowly down the stairs to the hall, where Aunt Tabby was waiting with his thermos and sandwiches. She kissed him goodbye and waved him off to work. The front door closed quietly behind him, and Aunt Tabby disappeared back down to the basement.

I slipped outside and changed the sign again. Now it said:

This
~~HAUNTED~~ House
Is ~~NOT~~
for Sale

That was sure to do it. Who would want to buy a haunted house?

~4~

SIR HORACE

Saturday morning was not a great morning. Aunt Tabby was cleaning the boiler—again. Usually I stay out of the way when Aunt Tabby goes anywhere near the boiler, but today was different. I wanted to collect new supplies of flour for my ghost box, as I thought I might be needing it soon, and Aunt Tabby keeps all her flour in the third-pantry-on-the-left-just-past-the-boiler-room.

I had nearly passed the boiler room safely when Aunt Tabby looked up and saw me. Drat. I could see she was going to be trouble. She had a big sooty scrubbing brush in her hand, and she had just kicked over a bucket of water.

I was right; she *was* trouble.

"Araminta *dear*," said Aunt Tabby, "will you *please* go and put Sir Horace back together. He has spent two whole days in pieces now."

Sir Horace? Since when has Aunt Tabby bothered about *Sir Horace*?

"Do I *have* to?" I asked, annoyed. I had better things to do than put a heap of rusty junk back together. Why was Aunt Tabby always popping up when you least wanted to see her?

"Yes, you *do* have to." Aunt Tabby kicked

the grate. "There are some people coming who want to buy the house, and I think a nice suit of armour in the hall will make a good impression. People like suits of armour. And Araminta—"

"What?" I said.

"I want everything left nice and tidy, *please!* The people are coming this afternoon."

"This afternoon?" I gasped. "But that doesn't give me nearly enough time to—" Oops.

"To what?" asked Aunt Tabby suspiciously, peering at me through her sooty spectacles.

"To . . . er . . . clean up my room," I told her in my nicest voice.

"Well, you had better get a move on then, hadn't you, dear?" said Aunt Tabby. "And take that awful old helmet back up with you."

I picked up Sir Horace's helmet and got

out of Aunt Tabby's way. Not *more* people coming to see the house, I thought. Couldn't they read the sign outside?

I went out into the garden to see if Aunt Tabby had changed the sign, but she hadn't. It still said:

I didn't understand it. Why would anyone want to buy a haunted house? But just to make sure, I added a bit more to the sign:

This HORRIBLE HAUNTED House Is ~~NOT~~ for Sale

I dumped Sir Horace's helmet on the floor in my Saturday bedroom—which is my favourite, as you can only get to it by climbing up a rope ladder and then squeezing through a small door, which keeps Aunt Tabby out. The trouble was, the rest of Sir Horace still lay all over the floor of my Thursday bedroom, so it took for ever to bring all the pieces down the corridor and then throw them up through the door. I am a pretty good shot, but I have to admit that not all the pieces got through the door the first time.

I started to put Sir Horace back together and, while I was working out which arm went where, I thought about my Plans for the afternoon. I thought that maybe I would try the Treacle on the Doorknob with the Invisible Tripwire Plan, although it might

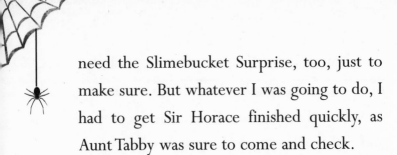

need the Slimebucket Surprise, too, just to make sure. But whatever I was going to do, I had to get Sir Horace finished quickly, as Aunt Tabby was sure to come and check.

Sir Horace was really difficult to put back together. There were even more dents in him now, and lots of the pieces wouldn't go back where they were meant to, no matter how hard I pounded them. It was *very* irritating.

It was nearly lunchtime by the time I had put Sir Horace back together—all, that is, except for his left foot. His left foot was just about the most stupid left foot I have ever known.

I was feeling very cross, so I told Sir Horace exactly what was what.

"It's all right for you, Sir Horace, you mouldy old rust bucket," I said, "but I've got much more important things to do. If I don't get my Plans ready, then some really *stupid* people who can't even read a perfectly *obvious* sign are going to buy this house, and we will have to move out. And when we do, Aunt Tabby is going to throw *you* in the recycling bin. And then you'll be taken away and squashed flat like a pancake and melted down and made into hundreds of tins—which will probably be filled up with cat food. Ha-ha."

By now I was really annoyed with his left foot. I banged it upside down on the floor and it rattled. I shook it again, and then something really exciting happened—a small brass key fell out.

I could tell it was a very old key, as it was worn quite smooth as if it had been in someone's pocket for hundreds of years. But the best part was that it had an old brown label tied to it, and on the label was some faint spidery writing in very old-fashioned letters. I could just about read what it said:

This be the keye to Balconie (Doth Fitt all Doors)

"Balconie" was a funny word, and I wondered what it meant. It sounded like a faraway land or an ancient underground city. Maybe, I thought, the key belonged to a treasure chest on a desert island called Balconie. I said the word out loud to myself, imagining the palm trees swaying and the water lapping at my feet, and then I realised what Balconie was. It was only the boring old balcony above the hall. And who would want to go *there*?

Me! That's who. Suddenly I knew it was the *perfect* place. I could do my Awful Ambush from there. And I've always wanted to do an Awful Ambush. It has just about everything in it, and it would make the Slimebucket Surprise look like a Sunday school picnic. Anyone coming to buy the house wouldn't last five seconds.

I gave one last shove to Sir Horace's left foot and—yes!—it went back on to the end of his leg. So what if it was on back to front? It didn't seem to bother Sir Horace, and it certainly didn't bother me. I had more important things to think about. Like how to get to the balcony. Of course, I knew there was only one answer to that—through a secret passage.

~5~
THE SECRET PASSAGE

I have a Secret Passage Kit, just like my Ghost Kit. I have always wanted to find a secret passage, and now I was sure that at last I had the key to one.

First I opened my Secret Passage Kit box and took out a torch, a ball of string and some emergency supplies of cheese and onion crisps. You need a torch because secret passages are always dark, and you need a ball

of string so that you can find your way out again—I'll tell you how that works in a minute. You need emergency food supplies as you never know how long you are going to be in the secret passage, do you? I mean it might be a really long one, and you could be in there for days. Weeks, even.

Then I set off to look for the secret door. I thought that the most likely place was in the wood panelling under the stairs. It sounds hollow when you kick it. But finding the door wasn't as easy as I thought it might be, as everything was covered in Aunt Tabby's favourite thick brown paint. When I looked really hard, I was sure I could see a keyhole-shaped dip. I scraped off the paint with the end of the key and there it was—a small brass keyhole just the right size for the small brass key. It fitted perfectly. So I turned the key and the best thing *ever* happened—a secret door swung open.

I switched on my torch and shone it through the doorway. It looked exactly like a secret passage should look—dark, dusty and really, really secret. You could tell that no one had been in there for years. Weird, I thought, because now *I* was going in. On my own. I'm not saying that I wished Aunt Tabby was there with me just then, as she was the last person

I wanted to see, but I wouldn't have minded a friend or someone like that. I don't want you to think that I was frightened of going in on my own, as I am quite used to doing stuff on my own and it is perfectly OK. No problem at all.

Here's the thing about the string. When you go into a secret passage, you have to tie one end of a ball of string to something and then you unwind the string as you go, so that you can always find your way back again. There was a nail on the back of the secret door, so I tied the string to that. Perfect. Then I closed the door so that Aunt Tabby didn't notice anything unusual, switched on my torch, and set off along the passage, unwinding the string as I went.

The secret passage was really strange. It

was very narrow and full of cobwebs and it smelled funny, kind of damp and mouldy. I think it ran behind the wooden panelling of the landing, as it had really scratchy wooden walls. Although it was narrow, it was quite high and easy to walk along, even though I had to keep pushing really thick cobwebs out of the way. It's a good thing I don't mind spiders, as there were dozens of *those*. Really fat ones.

I wasn't scared. Not really. After all, I was still in my house, wasn't I? But it was a bit odd when the passage suddenly ended at a wooden platform. I wasn't sure whether to step on to the platform or not. Anyone who knows about secret passages has heard about booby traps and stuff like that, so I stopped and thought about what to do. I shone my torch all around, but it wasn't much help. When I looked more closely, I could see that the platform had sides, a bit like a packing case, and there were ropes running up and down on either side. It reminded me of something, but I couldn't think what. And then I could!

It was a dumb waiter.

No, I am not being rude about some poor old waiter—a dumb waiter is a kind of lift. I knew that because there used to be one just like it in the first-kitchen-on-the-right-just-past-the-laundry-room, and that is what Aunt Tabby used to call it. I remember one rainy day I was *so* bored and I got inside the lift and hauled myself up to the dining room. It was the best fun ever, and I spent all afternoon going up and down until Aunt Tabby caught me. After that she nailed a load of planks across it so that I couldn't go in it any more, which I thought was mean.

So I stepped on to the platform and pulled on the rope, just as I had before. The platform kind of groaned a bit, but nothing happened. I put my torch down and used two hands to pull the rope really hard—and the platform moved! I suppose that *was* a little bit scary, as the platform started going down into what felt like a dark chimney, and I wasn't sure where I was heading. I was pretty pleased when I saw the top of an old door appear.

I stopped the platform outside the door. I could tell it was a very old door, as it had big iron hinges across it and looked as though it had come out of a castle or something. But I couldn't see a handle and, when I pushed it, it wouldn't move. Stupid door. I gave it a really big push, I even kicked it, but nothing happened. It just wouldn't budge.

Then I remembered what it said on the label on the little brass key— " *Doth Fitt all Doors.* "

I didn't really believe the key would fit, as it was so small compared with the door, but when I looked carefully I saw a small brass keyhole, just like the one on the door to the secret passage. The key turned easily, and the door swung open.

I shone my torch through the doorway, and it lit up a tiny room. The room had a small fireplace, some very dark and dusty pictures, and some big old candles in brass holders on the walls. In one corner there was a broken old chair with some tattered books piled up on it, and on the floor in front of the fireplace was an old rug. I just stood there for a moment, kind of holding my breath. It was so quiet that I hardly dared go in.

But I did.

I tiptoed in and swung my torch around the walls, looking for a door to the balcony. Of course there were no windows, but you wouldn't expect any in a secret room in the

very middle of a house, would you? But sure enough, there was a door. Great, I thought. It took me three steps to cross the room. I put the small brass key in the door and it swung open. I nearly walked straight out, as I really wanted to get to the balcony by then, because time was getting on, but I knew that you always have to look where you're going in a secret passage. It's a good thing I did, as the door opened out into *nothing*. A great big deep hole, in fact. Scary.

A gust of warm, musty wind blew up from the hole. It smelled kind of sooty and damp at the same time. I shone my torch and saw that there was an old wooden ladder leading down to . . . where?

But I didn't want to go down the ladder; I wanted to find the balcony. So I went back into the room and did all the things you have to do to make a secret door appear. I tried to turn the brass candlesticks, but they wouldn't move. I looked behind all the old pictures, but there was nothing there. I even kicked the old fireplace, but it felt as solid as a rock. There was no way out to the balcony—that was for sure.

So I decided to climb down the ladder.

It was a bit scary getting on to the ladder. It wobbled and creaked a lot, but I knew that you have to expect these things in a secret passage. Then the door slammed, and I nearly fell off. That was really scary.

I set off down the ladder, which was quite difficult as I could only hold on to it with one hand, since I had my torch in the other hand—and the ball of string in my teeth. I don't like the taste of string.

The other thing I didn't like very much was the way the air was getting hotter and hotter. I remembered about how it gets hotter as you get near the centre of the earth, and the more I climbed down the ladder, the more I wondered if I was getting too close to that bit in the middle where all the rocks melt. But just as I was wondering whether to go back up, I got to the bottom of the ladder and stepped on to the ground. It seemed pretty solid to me, so I guessed I hadn't got to the molten rock just yet.

I was in a real tunnel now, with brick sides and a sandy floor. I decided to follow the tunnel just for a while, in case the balcony was round the next corner. The tunnel twisted and turned all over the place, and the air became even hotter, which didn't make any sense to me, as I wasn't going down any more.

And then I heard it—a really horrible, teeth-grating, toe-curling, clanging noise. The exact kind of noise that you get when a ghost drags a ball and chain behind it. I have heard that those ball-and-chain ghosts are not nice ghosts to meet. I suppose they are grumpy because they have to drag all that stuff with them wherever they go. I stopped where I was and switched off my torch so that the ball-and-chain ghost would not see me, but being in the dark didn't make me feel any better. In fact, it made me feel a whole lot worse, so I switched the torch on again.

That was when the screaming started. Horrible, spine-chilling screaming. It filled up the secret passage and echoed all around me. It was the scariest sound I had ever, *ever* heard.

And the worse thing was, I knew for sure what it meant—that the ball-and-chain ghost was coming to get me.

EDMUND

Aunt Tabby may think it is a big joke to go around frightening people who are exploring secret passages, but I do not. In fact, I think it is in very poor taste, as Uncle Drac would say.

It did not take me long to realise that ball-and-chain ghosts do not scream, "BOTHER THIS BOILER!" In fact, I don't think that ball-and-chain ghosts are even a

little bit interested in boilers.

"BOTHER THIS BOILER! I HATE THIS GRATE!" I could hear Aunt Tabby yelling through the wall of the secret passage as clearly as if I was standing next to her. I was glad I wasn't standing next to her, as I could also hear her kicking the coal scuttle and throwing the shovel at the wall.

But time was running out. Soon a whole load of people who liked haunted houses would be walking around my house, deciding that *they* were going to live there instead of *me*. And if I was not careful, I would be stuck in a secret passage and not able to do a thing about it. I decided I had to give up on the balcony idea and go back and plan a Slimebucket Surprise. It was better than nothing.

Since Aunt Tabby had given me a really big fright, I wanted to give her one back before I went. I looked for a chink in the wall to shine my torch through so that she would think there was a ghost in the boiler room—and that was when I saw him.

I saw a ghost.

He was sitting in a dark corner a bit further down the secret passage. At first I was so surprised that I thought he was just an ordinary boy, so I said, "Hey! What are you doing here?"

But when he looked up at me, there was something about his face that made me shiver, and I knew he must be a ghost. He had watery, ghostly eyes, and his face was kind of transparent and glowed with a pale light. I thought he was probably a ghost from long ago, as he had a funny pudding basin haircut and wore a tunic with a long hood. He had a dagger tucked into his belt too, which I thought looked pretty good— Aunt Tabby won't let me have a dagger, however much I ask her. In fact, I felt as though I had seen him somewhere before, as he looked just like the pictures of medieval pages in my knight-time storybook.

I was pleased that he wasn't a nasty ball-and-chain ghost. I went up to him and asked, just to make sure, "Are you a *real* ghost?"

He didn't answer—in fact he looked

scared, like *he* had seen a ghost. It was a bit disappointing, really, as that was kind of back to front. *I* was meant to be scared of *him*.

"So what's your name?" I asked.

He still didn't answer, which I thought was rude. Aunt Tabby would have told him it was rude too. He looked away and stared at the floor, and I could tell he was hoping that I would just go away. But there was no way I was going to walk away from the very first ghost I had ever found, especially after I'd been looking for one for such a long time.

"You must have a *name*," I told him. I had expected a ghost to be more fun than this one was turning out to be. But then I heard something that made the hairs on the back of my neck stand up. A weird, hollow whisper filled up the air all around me.

"**Edmund** . . ." the whisper said. It was *him*—the ghost boy—talking. And it was *spooky*.

Edmund floated up from the floor and drifted over towards me. I took a step back, as I suddenly wasn't so sure that I wanted to talk to a ghost after all. And then Edmund said something really odd—he said, "**Are you the Tabitha?**"

He spoke with a strange accent that reminded me of some French people who had once turned up at the house, thinking it was a guesthouse. They hadn't stayed long.

"No," I told him, "I'm the . . . I'm Araminta."

"**Good,**" said Edmund, and he sort of walked up the wall and began to wander upside down along the ceiling. **"I do not like the Tabitha,"** he said in his funny accent. **"The Tabitha is noisy."**

He had a point, I thought. There were times when I didn't like the Tabitha either, and the Tabitha was most definitely noisy. In fact, just as Edmund was saying that, I could hear Aunt Tabby angrily shovelling coal into the boiler and banging the door closed with a loud clang. I reckoned Edmund must have heard a lot of Aunt Tabby's tantrums over the years.

Then, just as I was beginning to like Edmund, he said, **"You must go now."**

"What?" I asked him.

"You must go. You may not come any closer."

"Why?"

He didn't answer. He just floated up and

down in front of me with his arms out-
stretched, as if he could stop me from going
past him. He need not have bothered, as
there was no way I was going to walk through
a ghost. *Brrr.* No way at all.

"Well, I don't want to go any further, so
there," I told him. "I only came to look for the
way to the balcony."

"**The balcony is not down here,**" said
Edmund, who had begun slowly spinning

around for some weird reason—don't ask me why. **"So you must leave. Farewell."**

It sounded to me as though Edmund knew where the balcony was, so I asked him if he would take me there.

"If I take you to the balcony, will you go away?" he asked.

I don't hang around where I'm not wanted. I have better things to do.

"Well, I don't want to stay down here, do I?" I told him.

"Don't you?" said Edmund. **"Oh good. Follow me."**

So I followed him.

~7~

THE BALCONY

Edmund glowed really brightly, so I switched off my torch to conserve the batteries. Conserving your batteries is something you should always think about in a secret passage, as you never know how long you might be there, and it is the worst disaster ever to be in a secret passage with no light.

I followed Edmund floating along the

passage, and I thought about Aunt Tabby on the other side of the wall and how she would have a fit if she knew what I was doing right then—but not as much of a fit as she was going to have when I sprang my Awful Ambush from the balcony.

Soon I was climbing back up the rickety old ladder while Edmund just floated up in front of me. I thought how much easier it was for a ghost to go up ladders than an ordinary person. It didn't seem fair somehow, espe-cially as I had to carry my torch *and* wind up my ball of string as I went.

When we got to the top, Edmund stopped outside the door.

"Go on," I told him. I couldn't see why he had stopped, as everyone knows that ghosts can go right through doors.

"This door is difficult," he said. "I should not come here. It is not my room."

"It's all right," I said. "I've got the key."

Edmund sounded surprised. "You have the key?" he kind of murmured, and he began to shimmer and flicker. Then suddenly he was gone—straight through the door. And I was left stuck at the top of a horrible old ladder in the dark. Great. After fiddling around with the key for ages, I unlocked the door and kind of fell into the room. Edmund was floating there, just looking at me in a really unhelpful way.

"So where exactly *is* the balcony then?" I asked as I picked myself up.

Edmund pointed to the fireplace. "It is through there."

"Well, that's just stupid," I told him.

"How do I get through a fireplace? It's all very well for *you*. You're a ghost, but I can't just walk through a sooty old fireplace just like that—"

"You talk just like the Tabitha," said Edmund. "You make my ears hurt. Where is the key?"

"What key?" I asked crossly.

"The key to the balcony," he said as though I was really stupid or something. "The one you carry upon your person."

"Upon my *what?*" I said, and then I realised what he meant and fished the key out of my pocket. "Here you are," I said, and gave it to him. Of course it just dropped straight through his hand and fell on to the floor. Duh. I had forgotten for a moment that Edmund was a ghost, since he was being just as irritating as a real boy.

"**Place the key in the keyhole,**" said Edmund, and he waved his hand at a small keyhole in the middle of the fireplace that I hadn't noticed before. "**For it opens the way to the balcony. Farewell.**" Then he shot off through the door and disappeared.

I put the key in the

keyhole and turned it. It worked! The fire-place slid sideways, and a brilliant beam of sunlight pierced the room. I squeezed through the opening and there I was at last—on the balcony.

It was weird standing miles above the hall.

Everything looked so small and far away. I suppose that is what birds feel like all the time when they hang around in the big old trees out in the garden. I was so pleased that I was on the balcony at last that I very nearly yelled out to Aunt Tabby to come and see where I was—luckily, I stopped myself just in time.

But the best thing of all was that when I looked down, I could see the balcony was right above the floor in front of the doormat where people who have never been to the house always stop and stare. They often have their mouths open too, although they never seem to say much—and I have known them to stay like that for quite a long time.

It was perfect. Araminta's Awful Ambush was going to be the *best*.

I zoomed back up in the dumb waiter and
along the secret passage, but when I pushed
open the little door under the stairs, someone was waiting for me.

~8~

SIR HORACE

G uess who it was? No, not Aunt Tabby.
No, it wasn't Uncle Drac, either.

It was Sir Horace.

"Good morning!" he said in a really strange, booming voice that came from somewhere inside his suit of armour. It sounded so spooky that I got covered in goose pimples all over and my knees felt funny.

"G-good morning, Sir Horace," I gulped. I

considered making a run for it back down the secret passage, but I didn't think my legs would work very well.

Sir Horace loomed over me and looked very wobbly. I edged away, as I didn't think much of his chances of staying in one piece for very long—since it was me who had put him back together—and I could do without a rusty chunk of armour landing on me just then.

I thought that perhaps I had better try and explain things. I know explaining things doesn't always help, especially if the person you are explaining to is Aunt Tabby, but I thought Sir Horace might be different. So I said in my best polite voice, "Er . . . I'm very sorry, Sir Horace. But I . . . er . . . I thought you were just a . . . um . . ."

"A moldy old rust bucket," Sir Horace finished my sentence for me, which Aunt Tabby says is very rude.

"Ah . . ." I mumbled, trying to remember what else I had called Sir Horace when I was putting him back together. In fact, I still thought he *was* a mouldy old rust bucket,

but I hadn't expected him to be a *talking* rust bucket.

I thought I had better check out the ghost situation with Sir Horace, so I asked him, "Are you a ghost as well?"

"**As well as what?**" he boomed. "**Ah—as well as being a knight of the realm, you mean. Why yes, Miss Spook, indeed I am a ghost. The ghost of Sir Horace Harbinger of Hernia Hall, at your service.**" He made a sweeping bow. Three bolts fell from his neck and rattled down the stairs.

Wow. That meant he was my *second* ghost that morning—what were the chances of that? Of course, it was typical, I thought. I spend years looking for a ghost and then two come along at once, and just as Aunt Tabby is about to throw me and Uncle Drac out of the house, too.

But it all made sense to me now. Sir Horace never stayed in the same place for very long, and I had always thought that Aunt Tabby moved him around at night as a sort of joke. It would be just the sort of stupid joke that Aunt Tabby would like. But now I understood—Sir Horace moved *himself* around.

"I'm really sorry about your helmet—er . . . I mean, your head," I said, trying not to remember how I had kicked it all the way down the stairs. I hoped he didn't remember either.

"Got a terrible headache," said Sir Horace.

"Oh. Yes, well I suppose you would have," I said sympathetically.

"Walking's not too easy either," he said. We both looked down at his left foot, which was still jammed on back to front.

"Er . . . no, I can see it might not be," I said in my best helpful voice.

"**But**"—he boomed and kind of rattled at the same time—"**that is not what is bothering me. What is bothering me is this house-selling business.**"

"Oh, good," I told him, "because that's bothering *me*, too."

Sir Horace swayed a bit, and I dodged an old spring as it flew off his neck and pinged on to the floor. "**And this . . . cycling thing,**" he said.

For a moment I was confused, as I was sure I had never seen Sir Horace out on a bike. And then I realised what he meant.

"You mean *re*cycling," I told him.

"**Do I?**" he boomed. "**Well, don't like the**

sound of it, whatever it's called. Never did care for tins myself. Impossible to open. Can't stand cat food." And then, with a horrible teeth-on-edge creaking noise, Sir Horace stood up as straight as he could—which was not very straight at all—and took a deep breath. **"Something,"** he boomed so loud that I was afraid Aunt Tabby would hear, **"something must be done. This house must not be sold!"**

"Exactly!" I agreed. "And I've got a really *great* idea. I'm going to do my Awful Ambush from the balcony and—"

"From *my* balcony?" he interrupted. **"In *my* room?"**

Oops—so it was *Sir Horace's* room. And it seemed like he didn't like anyone going in there. I could understand how he felt, as I don't like Aunt Tabby going into any of my bedrooms either. She always manages to mess something up.

I thought I ought to explain. "I'm sorry, Sir Horace, but I found the key in your foot, and—" but he interrupted *again*.

"**I know**," he said, wiggling his left foot about as though he had pins and needles in it—which I knew for sure he didn't, as I had already emptied it out and all I had found was the key. "**I remember that very well. I had my head back on by then.**"

"I'm *really* sorry," I said. "Would you like your key back?"

Sir Horace shook his head very slowly, and it made a horrible grinding noise, like a pepper mill.

"Please keep the key, **Miss Spook**," he said. "I would be very pleased for you to use my balcony for your Awful Ambush. I myself have done many Awful Ambushes from there in years gone by. They can be very effective. I will ask my faithful page, Edmund, to assist you."

Aha. So *that* was who Edmund was, I thought. "Thank you very much, Sir Horace," I said.

"**You are most welcome, Miss Spook**," he replied, and bowed low.

"Careful!" I shouted, but it was too late. Sir Horace's head fell off and rolled along the corridor. I caught it just as it started bouncing down the stairs, but unfortunately Aunt Tabby saw me as she was attacking some spiderwebs on the landing below.

"Haven't you put Sir Horace back together

yet, Araminta?" she snapped at the same time as she made a hundred spiders homeless. Aunt Tabby likes making spiders and people homeless.

"Nearly finished, Aunt Tabby," I told her, and I rushed back to find Sir Horace. He was sitting on the bottom step looking surprised. Well, I think that was how he was looking, although it was hard to tell. I put his head back on. I was more careful this time, and I

could tell it had gone on the right way as there was a little click when it settled on to his shoulders.

"Ooh, that's better," he said. "That crick in my neck has completely gone." He moved his head about, and it didn't make the pepper mill noise any more. I felt pleased.

Then he hung on to the banister and heaved himself up, so that he was standing almost straight, and he said, "Well, jolly good, then, Miss Spook. You do your ambush and leave the rest to me."

"Great," I said.

"Right ho. And tell young Edmund I said to provide you with all necessary assistance. Until we meet again, Miss Spook." He started to bow, but then he changed his mind. He walked away, kind of lurching from side to side until he reached a dark corner on the landing and propped himself up in it.

This was turning out to be good day after all—a secret passage, two ghosts, and one Awful Ambush coming up. What could be better?

~9~

AMBUSH KIT

You need a lot of stuff for an Awful Ambush. And most of the things I needed were—*bats.* Lots and lots of bats.

So I went off to Uncle Drac's turret to catch as many as I could. I'm pretty good at catching bats, as I always help Uncle Drac with them whenever they escape. Aunt Tabby hates bats. She thinks that they are going to nest in her hair, but no self-respecting bat would want to go anywhere near Aunt Tabby's hair, as it is stuffed full of hairpins. They would be bat-kebabs in five seconds flat.

Anyway, I found my bat sack and soon I was crawling very carefully along a rafter at the top of the turret. Uncle Drac was fast asleep, snoring in his sleeping bag, which hung from the rafters and swayed with each snore. There was a crowd of bats fast asleep all around him, although I don't think the bats were snoring. Or perhaps I just couldn't hear them. Maybe bat snores are too high-pitched for humans to hear.

"Here, bats," I whispered, and scooped up as many as I could and stuffed them into the sack. The bats didn't mind; they *liked* my bat sack. Well, all except Big Bat, who does not

like *anything*, as he is a grumpy old bat. But I really wanted to have Big Bat in the ambush since I reckoned he would be pretty scary.

I grabbed him when he wasn't looking, and he squeaked really loudly.

Uncle Drac stopped snoring and snuffled a bit in his sleeping bag, and I froze. I really didn't want him to wake up, as I knew he would not let me have any of his precious bats, even if they were going to save the house from a lot of stupid people who wanted to take it away from us. Uncle Drac's bats are more important to him than anything else in the world.

When I had enough bats, I took them all down to Sir Horace's room and left them roosting in the dark. They looked really happy.

The next thing I needed for the Awful Ambush Kit was . . . *strawberry jelly*. This was more difficult, as I had to go back into Aunt

Tabby's territory. I had to get to the fourth-kitchen-on-the-right-just-past-the-boiler-room. I zoomed by the boiler room at top speed, and I didn't see Aunt Tabby anywhere, although there was a large pile of soot in the corner, so I knew she'd be around soon to sweep it up.

In no time at all, I was in the fourth-kitchen-on-the-right-just-past-the-boiler-room and had found what I was looking for—a giant box of mix for Extra-Sticky Strawberry Jelly. I had made two buckets full of strawberry jelly and was slowly slopping my way along the basement corridor with them when, sure enough, I heard Aunt Tabby.

"Is that you, dear?" she called out. I don't like it when Aunt Tabby says "dear" like that, through gritted teeth. It always means trouble.

I sped up as fast as I could, but it was too late. You can never escape Aunt Tabby, however hard you try. As I splashed past the open door to the boiler room, the large pile of soot spoke to me.

"Well done, dear," said the pile of soot. "It's very sweet of you to clean your bedrooms. It makes such a difference if people see a nice clean house. I just hope they get to see a nice clean boiler as well."

The pile of soot shook itself, and I could see it was really Aunt Tabby with a broom.

"You know, I have a funny feeling that these people will be just right for the house," she said.

I stomped off with my buckets. "Funny feeling," I muttered. "I'll show them a funny feeling all right."

I soon had all the other stuff for the Awful Ambush. I had:

- a large bag of assorted spiders
- a big pile of pillowcases
- a massive tub of strangled ghost squealers
- a huge box of balloons
- a giant bag of flour

I took it all down to Sir Horace's room and dumped it in a big pile in the middle of the floor. Phew. And then someone coughed. I jumped about six feet into the air and nearly fell into a bucket of Extra-Sticky Strawberry Jelly.

"**Hello,**" said Edmund.

"You shouldn't go creeping up on people like that," I told him, "especially if you are a ghost. Someone could hurt themselves."

"**But Sir Horace told me to come and help you,**" Edmund said. "**He said that there were some people coming who were going to put him in a dustbin with some bicycles and make him into cat food. But I do not understand why they wish to do this.**"

"It's because of the Tabitha," I told Edmund.

"**Ah,**" said Edmund, "**I see.**"

After that Edmund was really helpful.

First we got the "ghosts" ready— Edmund blew up the balloons and I put the squealers in. I tied a slip-knot around the ends so that I could set them off quickly. I put the balloons in the pillowcases and poured flour over them, then I opened the fireplace and Edmund wafted the "ghosts" out on to the balcony.

Next I scooped all the spiders out of the spider bag and hung them from the bars of the balcony. It was perfect—they dangled just above the place where people always stopped with their mouths wide open.

Last of all I carried out the buckets of Extra-Sticky Strawberry Jelly and set them up on the edge of the balcony.

We left the bats sleeping in Sir Horace's room until they were needed. Then Edmund and I sat down behind the buckets and waited.

We were ready for anything.

~10~
ARAMINTA'S AWFUL AMBUSH

We didn't have to wait long—soon someone was banging on the front door so hard that I was surprised the door didn't fall off, just like it did last week.

Aunt Tabby was at the top of the basement stairs in no time. She was still covered in soot, and she was looking around to see if I was going to try and race her to the front door like I usually do. She looked really

pleased when she realised I wasn't there, and she scurried across the hall like the biggest spider you have ever seen and pulled the front door open with a thump, spraying soot everywhere.

Standing on the doorstep was the weirdest bunch of people. Edmund stared at them as if he had never seen anything like them before in his life—which I suppose he hadn't, since he'd last been alive about five hundred years ago.

The first person on the doorstep was a short, round woman wearing sunglasses and a bright pink dress covered with big red spots. She was holding an extremely fat black cat. Who takes their cat with them to look at a house? Weird.

Next was a really tall, thin man. He was

wearing a bright green coat and long, yellow pointed boots covered in red stars. On his head he had a blue bowler hat with a small green frog on the top of it. I thought it was probably a stuffed frog until it hopped off his hat and landed on the smallest person on the doorstep. *She* looked really boring, and a little bit stupid. Well, quite a lot stupid, actually. She had short, mousy hair and was wearing a blue school top and a grey skirt. The only slightly interesting thing about her was the green frog that was now sitting on top of her head. But the green frog soon got bored too, and it hopped straight back on to the blue bowler hat.

Aunt Tabby looked at the weird people like they were the best things she'd seen all day.

"How lovely to see you," she cooed in her very best polite voice. "*Do* come in."

"Thank you," said the sunglasses woman. "So nice to meet you, Mrs . . . er?"

"Spook," said Aunt Tabby. "Tabitha Spook."

"I am Brenda Wizzard," said the sunglasses woman. "This is my husband, Barry, and our daughter, Wanda. We saw your *wonderful* sign and we'd *love* to buy your house."

"Great," said Aunt Tabby. "Do come in."

The weird people who wanted to steal my house walked into the hall and stood just where I expected them to stand—right under the balcony. Perfect. And then they did just what I expected them to do—they gazed around in amazement with their mouths wide open. Fantastic!

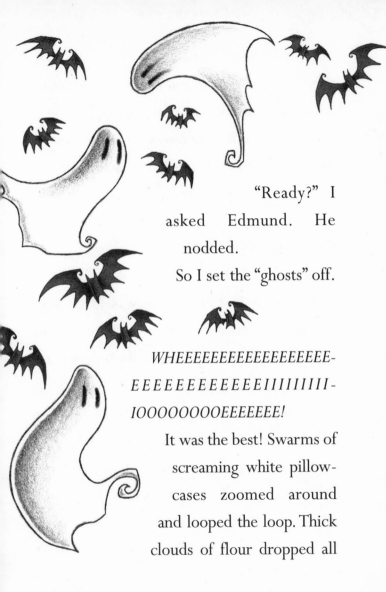

"Ready?" I asked Edmund. He nodded.

So I set the "ghosts" off.

WHEEEEEEEEEEEEEEEEEE-
EEEEEEEEEEEEIIIIIIIII-
IOOOOOOOOEEEEEEE!

It was the best! Swarms of screaming white pillow-cases zoomed around and looped the loop. Thick clouds of flour dropped all

over the weird people and then the pillowcases fell on their heads. One of them dropped right over the small boring one so that she looked like a ghost too. All you could see were her spindly little legs.

Then I tipped the buckets of Extra-Sticky Strawberry Jelly out.

SPLATTTTTTTTT!

It was perfect. The jelly was just right. Lumps of horrible, sticky red slime fell on their heads. It ran right down their necks and got stuck inside their clothes.

Then came the best part. Edmund woke up the bats and shooed them out of Sir Horace's room. They came out like a huge black cloud, and they went *everywhere*. The whole hall was just a storm of flapping bats. It was fantastic. Aunt Tabby screamed, almost as loudly as Huge Hotels had done. And while she was screaming, I cut the spiderwebs.

It rained spiders. Really fat ones. Hundreds of them fell on to the weird people. They got stuck in their hair, they dropped down their necks and got covered in Extra-Sticky Strawberry Jelly. They shot up their sleeves and trouser legs, trying to find somewhere safe to hide. A family of fifteen particularly hairy spiders fell on the sunglasses woman. I don't think she liked spiders much. She screamed really loudly too, and her cat leaped into the air and landed on Aunt Tabby's head. It was the best thing I'd seen all day.

But things got even better because, you see, Aunt Tabby is allergic to cats. *Really* allergic. They make her sneeze the hugest sneezes I have ever heard and give her big, red, scratchy bumps. It is not nice.

So Aunt Tabby sneezed—and when Aunt Tabby sneezes, she really goes for it. *"Ah-ah-aaaah-aaaaaaaaaaah-TISHOOOOOO!"*

She lost her balance, slipped on a pile of jelly, and hurtled into the sunglasses woman at full speed. The sunglasses woman toppled over like a falling tree and kind of clung on to Aunt Tabby as she went down. Then they both slid across the hall together, complete with the cat, which was still hanging on to Aunt Tabby's head.

Aunt Tabby sneezed again.

"A h - a h - a a a a h - a a a a a a a a a a a h - TISHOOOOOOOOO!"

The cat screeched and leaped up into the air. It was just amazing; I can still see it now, in slow motion. This great fat cat flying through the air with its hair standing up on end and its claws out, coming gracefully to land on a large puddle of Extra-Sticky Strawberry Jelly. It touched down beautifully, then it streaked across the hall, twirling around like an ice skater—and collided with Sir Horace.

Edmund told me later that Sir Horace had prepared a speech and was planning to deliver it to Aunt Tabby to make her see the error of her ways. He had been carefully clanking down the stairs ever since he had heard the weird people arrive, but no one had noticed him what with all the other stuff going on.

But they all noticed him now.

The cat cannoned into his left foot, which flew off and skittered across the floor. Then, with the most horrible noise and very slowly, piece by piece—just like a tower of cat food cans in the supermarket—Sir Horace collapsed into a rusty heap.

I peered over the balcony to see how the weird people were taking this. It looked promising. The smallest one was still struggling to get out of her pillowcase. The frog man was covered in bats, and the sunglasses woman was just lying on her back like a stranded beetle, staring up at the ceiling.

Aunt Tabby looked really, really angry. She got up, dusted herself off, then looked straight up at the balcony and said, "*Really*, Araminta. You have gone *too* far this time."

I didn't reply, as I was too busy looking at the sunglasses woman trying to get up. She did exactly what stranded beetles do—kind of waved her legs about, rolled over, and picked herself up. Then she scrabbled through the remains of Sir Horace and fished out her cat, which leaped at her and clung to her like a piece of Velcro.

I nudged Edmund, but my elbow went right through him and hit the balcony rail. Ouch. "You wait," I told him. "She'll be out the front door in five seconds flat."

But she wasn't. She just stood in the middle of the hall, gazing around her.

"Wonderful," she said. "This is our dream home!"

~11~

GO AWAY!

I could not believe it. There was the sun-glasses woman gazing into space like her best dream ever had just come true.

Then the frog man got up and waved a few bats away, and *he* said, "Perfect! It's even better than we expected, isn't it, dear?"

"It is," agreed the sunglasses woman. She turned to Aunt Tabby and shook her hand. "What a *wonderful* welcome," she said.

"Thank you *so* much."

And then the small boring one heaved herself out of the pillowcase and said in a really *stupid* squeaky voice, "I'd *love* to live here; it's *so* exciting." She tugged at the woman's sticky sleeve and pestered her, "Can we live here, Mum? Please, please, *please* can we, Mum?"

"Of course, dear." The sunglasses woman smiled.

Huh. I really don't think it is good to give in to children who pester, especially irritating ones with squeaky voices.

But the sunglasses woman went right ahead and said to Aunt Tabby, "This house is perfect. We'll take it. We can move in tomorrow!"

What? Now I really could *not* believe it. It had been the best Awful Ambush I could possibly have done. Everything had worked perfectly—even Sir Horace had turned up. But not only had the weird people *liked* it, it had made them *want* to buy the house. What more could I do? So I yelled at them.

"GO AWAY!" I shouted as loud as I could. It was great yelling from so high; it echoed around and around the hall, and everyone looked up. Three of them looked amazed and one looked annoyed. "You *can't* live here," I yelled at the top of my voice. "It's *my* house and *I* live here. *GO AWAY!*"

The annoyed one opened her mouth to say something, but I got in first. "It's all *your* fault, Aunt Tabby!" I told her. "You never asked me about selling the house, and you never asked Uncle Drac, either. You just *told* us what you had decided to do. It's *not* fair. We *all* live here, not just *you*. And I want to *stay* living here and I'm not going, I'm NOT!"

Aunt Tabby wiped the soot and flour and strawberry jelly and spiders off her face. "Well," she said, "making a disgusting mess doesn't exactly make me want to stay here, Araminta. The place is difficult enough to keep clean as it is. I suggest we all go and have a cup of tea and talk about it. I'm sure you'll feel better about things when you have talked to Mr and Mrs Wizzard."

The weird people followed Aunt Tabby

down the stairs to the kitchens. Just before they disappeared, the stupid short one looked up at the balcony. I stuck out my tongue and gave her my best Fiendish Stare. That showed her.

"What a twit," I said to Edmund.

And can you guess what Edmund said? It was *completely* idiotic. He said, **"I thought she looked all right."** *I thought she looked all right!* I couldn't believe what I was hearing. I gave him my Fiendish Stare as well, and he shot off into Sir Horace's room, but I followed him. I had a Last Chance Plan, and I needed Edmund's help.

"You've got to come down to the kitchen with me," I told Edmund, who had backed into a corner. "If they saw a *real* ghost, they wouldn't last five seconds."

"You said that before," Edmund said, in an irritating way, "and they're still here. Anyway, I think they're nice. I'd like them to stay."

"Look, Edmund," I told him, as he obviously had *not* got the point, "if *they* stay, *I* have to go. You wouldn't want that, would you?"

Well, that told *him*. He didn't say anything at all; he just floated off and headed for the rickety old ladder. But there was no way I was going to let him get away. "Edmund!" I yelled.

"What?" he said in a really grumpy voice.

"You're Sir Horace's page, aren't you?" I asked him.

"Yes . . ." he said.

"So—you're meant to do what he tells you, aren't you?"

"**Ye-es** . . ."

"And Sir Horace told you to help me, *didn't he?*"

"**Yes** . . ." He sighed just like Aunt Tabby does when the boiler has done something really annoying.

"Well, I need you to *help me* get rid of all those horrible people. Right now. I want you to come with me and scare them away."

"**All right**," said Edmund in a sulky voice.

But I didn't care how sulky he was. This was my Last Chance Plan, and it *had* to work.

~12~

THE LAST CHANCE PLAN

Uncle Drac was part of the Last Chance Plan as well. I could see that Edmund was probably not up to the job. It would be just like him to float off at the wrong moment, or not be scary enough. So I needed Uncle Drac, too, because I knew he would be on my side.

I was just about to open the little door to the bat turret when it flew open and Uncle

Drac fell out on to the landing.

"Oh, Minty, Minty," he said, "something terrible has happened. All my bats have gone."

"No they haven't," I told him.

"Yes they have. They've—"

"Uncle Drac," I said sternly, "while you've just been hanging up there asleep doing nothing but snore, Aunt Tabby has gone and *sold our house!*"

Uncle Drac looked confused. He doesn't like being awake during the day. "Wha-at?" he mumbled.

"There are three weird people here, Uncle Drac—and one of them is really yucky, you wouldn't believe it, she's *so stupid*—and Aunt Tabby *is selling them our house!*"

"Eh?" Uncle Drac can be really slow at

times. I just grabbed hold of him and pulled him along with me.

"You can come out now!" I yelled to Edmund, who had been sulking in the secret passage. He floated out.

"Who's that, Minty?" Uncle Drac asked me when he saw Edmund.

"That's Edmund, Uncle Drac. And if you can't get Aunt Tabby to change her mind about selling our house, he's going to scare those people away."

Uncle Drac kept looking behind him as Edmund followed us down the stairs. "He doesn't look very well, Minty. What's wrong with him?" he whispered.

"He's dead, Uncle Drac."

"Dead?" Uncle Drac suddenly looked as pale as Edmund.

"He's a *ghost*," I told him very patiently. "Now come on, *quick*, before Aunt Tabby sells the house and you have to start packing up all the bats."

"My bats. *Where* did you say my bats were, Minty?"

"I didn't, Uncle Drac. Just hurry up, please. *Both* of you."

How I got Edmund and Uncle Drac down to the third-kitchen-on-the-right-just-round-

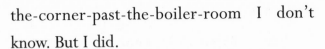

the-corner-past-the-boiler-room I don't know. But I did.

Everyone was sitting around the table, and Aunt Tabby was pouring some tea.

"Ah, Drac," said Aunt Tabby, looking up from the teapot. "I'm glad you're here. And Araminta. And, er—who's your friend, Araminta? He looks very pale. Would he like a hot drink?"

"This is Edmund," I told her. "And he wouldn't like anything, thank you. He's a ghost."

I looked around to see what effect that would have on the weird people, but they just gazed at Edmund and looked even more excited.

"Oh how *wonderful*," cooed the sunglasses woman. "A little boy ghost. He's so *sweet*.

Hello, Edmund dear."

"**Hello,**" whispered Edmund.

"Listen, Edmund," I hissed, "'Hello' is just not good enough. Can't you manage a blood-curdling howl or something?"

But Edmund didn't do anything. He just hovered by the door in a very boring and unscary way with a silly smile on his face. Being a ghost was wasted on Edmund, I thought. If I was a ghost, I'd have been howling around the kitchen, screeching and hurling all the things off the table—and that would have been just for starters.

The small Wizzard person was grinning at Edmund, so I made my wide-mouth frog face at her. But she just giggled. And then something really weird happened. She picked up the glass of orange juice that Aunt Tabby had just poured for her and suddenly it fizzed up over the glass and *turned blue*. For a moment I hoped that perhaps Aunt Tabby had had a change of heart and was trying to poison her, but the Wizzard man said, "Stop playing with your drink, Wanda."

Wanda clicked her fingers and changed it back to *orange* orange juice again. Show-off. Then she took four pet mice out of her pocket and put them on the table in front of her. The

mice started doing handstands and cartwheels around her glass. Double show-off.

Uncle Drac shuffled in past Edmund, and Aunt Tabby made him sit down next to her. "Drac dear," said Aunt Tabby, "this is Brenda, Barry and Wanda Wizzard, and they are going to buy our house. Isn't that lovely?"

Uncle Drac didn't say anything. He was looking at me—in fact *everyone* was looking at me—so I turned my wide-mouth frog face into my cross-eyed wide-mouth frog face.

Aunt Tabby sighed. "But as you can tell, Drac, Araminta's being a bit . . . difficult."

"Wait a minute, Tabby," mumbled Uncle Drac, blinking a bit. Uncle Drac has trouble seeing in the light, and sometimes I think he is like a great big bat himself. "Do we really *have* to sell the house?" he said. "Minty is very upset, and my bats are behaving very strangely."

"And so," Aunt Tabby told him, "is the boiler. As *usual*. And I am *not* putting up with that boiler *any more,* Drac. I *mean* it."

"Oh, dear," mumbled Uncle Drac.

I could see that Uncle Drac was going to let Aunt Tabby win—as usual—so I said, "Uncle Drac, you have to do something. *Please*."

"Do I?" he said, looking worried.

"Yes," I told him. "You *do*."

I sat down opposite him and looked at him. I didn't do a wide-mouth frog face or even a Fiendish Stare. I just looked at him like it was really important. Which it was.

Uncle Drac coughed a bit and then he said, "Tabby dear, I am sorry about the boiler. I do realise I have neglected it recently and left you to do all the work. I know it wasn't fair, and I promise that from now on I will share the boiler cleaning—"

"And the kindling chopping and the coal fetching," put in Aunt Tabby.

"Er, yes, and that too."

"And the emptying and the lighting and the—"

"Yes, yes, I'll do that as well."

"Promise?"

"Promise," said good old Uncle Drac.

Aunt Tabby sat down rather suddenly. "Well," she said, "I've had some shocks today, Drac, but having you offer to share all the boiler work is the biggest one so far."

"Does that mean you're not going to sell the house?" I asked Aunt Tabby.

"Yes, all right then, Araminta." Aunt Tabby sighed. "I'm not going to sell the house."

"Ya-ay!" I yelled.

"Oh," mumbled the Wizzard people.

"I'm very sorry," Aunt Tabby told them, "but the house is not for sale any more. Would you like another cup of tea?"

"No, thank you," said the Wizzard woman, sighing. "We had better be going."

About time, too, I thought—but she didn't get up. Instead she said, "Er, I couldn't help noticing that you had a model three with double ash bins and a reverse riddler. It is in fact one of the very rare B Series."

"A serious what?" asked Aunt Tabby.

"Your boiler. I wondered if I could take a little peek at it before I go. They are very unusual nowadays, you know." Aunt Tabby looked at the Wizzard woman like she was crazy, but she took her off to the boiler room even so.

When they'd gone, Uncle Drac heaved himself out of his chair. "Must go and find all my bats," he said.

"Need any help?" asked the Wizzard man. "They can be difficult to catch on your own."

"Thanks," said Uncle Drac, and he and the Wizzard man went off to find the bats.

"I too must take my leave," said Edmund, and he floated off through the kitchen wall.

"Bye, Edmund," said the show-off Wizzard girl.

"**Farewell, Wanda,**" said Edmund's voice from somewhere inside the wall.

That left me and the Wanda Wizzard girl together. "I could show you how to turn your orange juice blue if you like," she offered.

I thought she might as well. After all, you never know when a trick like that might come in handy, do you?

So I said, "OK."

~13~

WANDA AND ARAMINTA

Wanda wasn't as bad as she looked.

She showed me how to do blue orange juice fizz, and soon I had turned the tea *and* Uncle Drac's coffee blue as well and they were fizzing all over the place. But then Wanda said that she thought she ought to go. I said she could stay a bit longer and show me her mice doing handstands if she wanted, so we watched her mice do the Amazing Mouse

Pyramid, which was pretty good. Then we heard an enormous smash from upstairs, and we rushed up to see what was happening.

It was really funny. Wanda's dad, Barry, was swinging from the curtains trying to grab Big Bat, while Uncle Drac held a large net. Aunt Tabby's best vase was smashed on the floor. Oops.

"Hey, Big Bat!" Uncle Drac was yelling. "Come here, Big Bat, there's a good bat!"

Big Bat flew off, and Barry fell into the net.

Wanda and I laughed so much that we fell on to the floor, but Barry and Uncle Drac looked cross, so I took Wanda upstairs to see all my bedrooms. Wanda thought they were great, as she only had one bedroom at her home and that was really, really tiny.

After that, as Barry was still helping Uncle Drac catch Big Bat and Brenda was still looking at the boiler with Aunt Tabby, Wanda helped me put Sir Horace back together again. We cleaned off all the jelly and flour and polished him with some of Aunt Tabby's boiler polish. *And* we got his left foot back on properly.

Once he was all back together, Sir Horace got up and stretched. **"Gosh, that's done my back good,"** he said, and he squeaked off and propped himself up in a corner of the hall.

"He could do with some oil," said Wanda. "I've got some stuff for my bike that would work really well."

"Can you ride a bike?" I asked her. I have always wanted to have a bike, but Aunt Tabby says they are dangerous.

"Of course I can," said Wanda. "I could teach you if you like."

I thought Wanda was turning out to be quite interesting, all things considered.

Which is why, when Wanda's mum, Brenda, said, "Come on, Wanda, we really must go home now," I said, "Can Wanda stay the night, Aunt Tabby? Can she? Please please please please *please*?"

So Wanda stayed the night. And so did Brenda and Barry. Brenda wanted to get the boiler working properly, and Barry was still helping Uncle Drac catch Big Bat.

They stayed the next night as well. And the next, *and* the next, and the next. And then, this morning, Aunt Tabby said that it was silly for them to go home at all, unless they wanted to, and Brenda, Barry and

Wanda said no, they didn't really want to.

So I don't mind at all now that Aunt Tabby decided to sell the house, because it is much more fun with Wanda here, *and* I found two ghosts—so now I know that I really do live in a haunted house, just like I always wanted.

ANGIE SAGE, the celebrated author of the Septimus Heap series, shares her house with three ghosts who are quite shy. Two of the ghosts walk up and down the hall every now and then, while the other one sits and looks at the view out of the window. All three are just about the nicest ghosts you would ever wish to meet. She lives in Cornwall.

JIMMY PICKERING studied film and character animation and has worked for Hallmark, Disney and Universal Studios. He is the illustrator of several picture books.

www.aramintaspook.co.uk